THE PRINCESS AND THE WHITE BEAR KING

To love, the unending story, and to the Goldwater and Lush families who gave me a place to write, east of Auckland and west of the deep blue sea — T. R. B.

To my dear Aunt Luci — N. C.

Barefoot Books
2067 Massachusetts Avenue
Cambridge, MA 02140

First published in the United States of America in 2004 by Barefoot Books, Inc
This hardcover edition printed in 2008

This book was typeset in Bembo 14pt
The illustrations were prepared in acrylics, pencils and oil pastels on canvas

Graphic design by Louise Millar, London
Color separation by Bright Arts, Singapore
Printed and bound in China by Printplus Ltd

This book has been printed on 100% acid-free paper

ISBN 978-1-84686-228-1

Library of Congress Cataloging-in-Publication Data is available upon request

3 5 7 9 8 6 4

THE PRINCESS AND THE WHITE BEAR KING

retold by Tanya Robyn Batt
illustrated by Nicoletta Ceccoli

In the North, where the thickly-needled pine forests are deep and dark and the snow falls bride-white, there once lived three Princesses, daughters of a King and Queen. All three were beautiful, but with her long, fair hair and her dreamy eyes, the youngest was the fairest by far. And her father loved her best.

One night, the youngest Princess dreamt of a golden crown, and the gold of the crown was brighter than the sun itself. When she awoke, there was nothing she wanted more than to go back to sleep and keep company with her dream.

When the King heard about his daughter's dream, he ordered all his smiths and craftsmen to forge fine crowns. But some crowns were too big and others were too small; some were too intricate and others were too plain. None of the crowns made at her father's command were as fine as the one the Princess had dreamt about.

One day, as she was walking in the forest, the Princess came across a great bear, with a shaggy, snow-white pelt and huge paddle paws. He tossed into the air a crown of gold, the crown of the Princess's dream.

"Bear, give me that crown," the Princess cried.

"This crown is not for sale, not for gold or for money," he growled, "but I will give it to you in exchange for yourself."

The Princess agreed at once and the bear promised to fetch her in one week's time.

But when the bear came, the King barred the castle gate and set soldiers to guard it. The bear splintered the gate and knocked all the soldiers to the ground. And so the King sent out his eldest daughter. The Princess climbed upon the bear's great shaggy back. They rode and they rode over the bride-white snow and through the thickly-needled forest.

Then the bear called, "Are you afraid?"

"Yes!" cried the girl, and the bear shook her from his back. "Then you are not the one," he muttered. And he returned to the King's castle.

Now the King sent out his second daughter. She too rode far into the forest, until the bear growled, "Are you afraid?" And the girl trembled as she answered, "Yes." She too was thrown from the bear's back to the ground.

When the bear returned for a third time, the youngest Princess ran out to greet him. She clambered onto his back and buried her face in his thick white pelt.

They rode like the wind, through day and through night, over great frozen lakes and through dark forests until the bear called out, "Are you afraid?"

"No," whispered the Princess.

"Then you are the one," purred the bear.

They rode and they rode until they came to a magnificent castle, with white stone turrets and windows like eyes blinking in all directions. Treasures, trophies and lavish tapestries decked the walls and each magnificent room led into another. On a glass table in the center of one such room sat a small golden bell.

"You are free to use the castle as you please," the bear said in a low gentle rumble. "If there is anything you wish for, all you need do is ring the bell."

And with that he stroked her cheek with his paw, then lumbered away.

The Princess explored the castle until she grew heavy with sleep. When she rang upon the small golden bell she found herself lying in a great soft bed covered with a soft, pink quilt. Her eyes had hardly closed when she was stirred by the gentle padding of paws. She heard the sound of something soft but heavy falling to the floor, but she was too tired to worry about it. Soon, she was fast asleep.

And so time passed. Every day, the Princess found more to delight her in the castle grounds. And every night, she heard the gentle padding of paws as she drifted into sleep. Months ate days, and days ate hours, and with only the bear for company, generous though he was, she grew more and more lonely until one morning, she felt so very homesick that she asked the bear to take her back to her family — not for ever, but at least for one week.

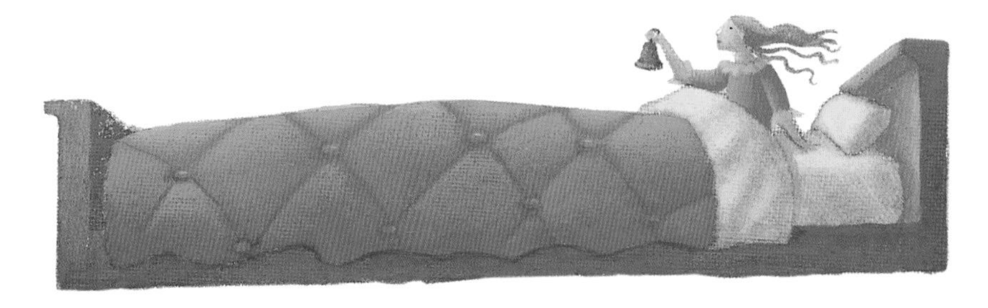

"This can be done," answered the bear, "but you must make me a promise. Do not listen to your mother's advice, for if you do, bad luck will befall us both."

The Princess promised she would do as he asked and so the bear carried her back through the thickly-needled forest to her father's castle. Her family greeted her with such joy, it was as if a hundred summers had come at once. For six days, the Princess remembered the bear's advice, and she took care to stay with her sisters so that her mother could not question her too closely. But on the seventh day, the Queen took her to one side and asked her how she spent her time at the castle, and the Princess told her about the magnificent castle, and about the strange sound she heard each night in her room as she fell asleep.

"It is some evil enchantment," whispered the Queen. "Maybe the bear is really a troll." Then she pressed a candle and a knife into her daughter's hand. "The next time you hear a sound, have this knife close, and light this candle so that you can see who it is."

The Queen's words lay heavy with the Princess, for she had trusted the bear, but now doubt poisoned her mind. So when the bear came to fetch her and carry her back to his castle, she carried hidden the candle and the knife. And when the bear asked her if she had listened to her mother's advice, she lied and said, "No."

That night, when the Princess heard the tread of the soft paddle paws and the sound of something soft and heavy falling to the ground, she lit the candle to see who was there. To her astonishment, it was no troll that she saw, but a young man so beautiful that she trembled with shame, and as she did so, she spilled hot wax from the candle on his shirt.

The beautiful young man stared at the Princess with such sadness in his eyes that she could not return his gaze. "What have you done?" he cried. "Know now the ill luck you have brought upon us both. Had you but waited until a year had passed, the enchantment put upon me by the Troll Queen would have been broken, and I would have become the Prince that I was born to be, and your own true love. But now I must leave you and travel to a land east of the sun and west of the moon and marry the Troll Queen. And you and I shall never again be together, for there is nothing I can do now to break the enchantment."

And with that he wrapped his great white pelt about him and fell to all fours, a bear.

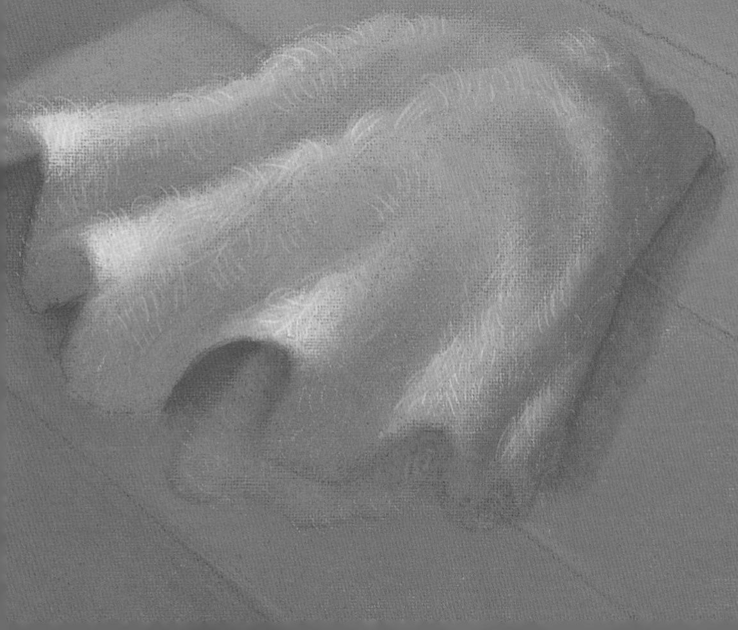

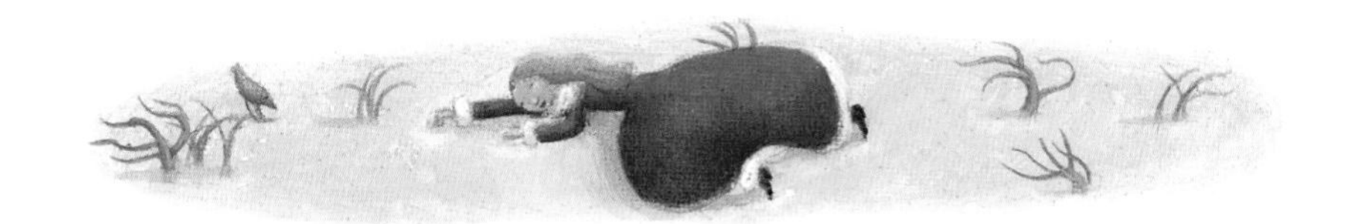

The Princess threw herself upon his back and cried that he might take her with him, but the bear was deaf to her cries. He ran out into the night and through the forest, and he would not stop. The Princess clung to his fur until she was so scratched and so numb with cold that she fell exhausted onto the forest floor.

When she awoke she was all alone, with forest and snow stretching in all directions. So she stood up and walked through the great snowdrifts. She walked and she walked, until she thought she could walk no further. Then one evening, she saw at last the lights of a lonely cottage.

The Princess knocked politely on the door and was invited in by an old woman.

"Pardon me, mother," said the Princess, "but have you seen a great white bear, heading for a land that lies east of the sun and west of the moon? I think he might have passed this way."

The old woman nodded, "Here he came and now he's gone. That way he went, but you'll never catch him." She pointed toward the thick of the forest.

"There I go, late or never," the Princess sighed and as she turned to leave the old woman called out, "If you are traveling to the land that lies east of the sun and west of the moon, you had better take this with you," and she handed the Princess a tablecloth. The Princess thanked her and tucked it into the folds of her skirt.

She walked and she walked for a year and a day, until she came upon a second cottage. There sat an old woman carding wool.

"Pardon me, mother," said the Princess, "but have you seen a great white bear, heading for a land that lies east of the sun and west of the moon? I think he might have passed this way."

The old woman nodded, "Here he came and now he's gone. That way he went, but you'll never catch him." The old woman pointed into the thick of the forest.

"There I go, late or never," the Princess sighed and as she turned to leave the old woman called out, "If you are traveling to the land that lies east of the sun and west of the moon, you had better take this with you." And she handed the Princess a pair of silver scissors. The Princess thanked her and tucked the gift into the folds of her skirt.

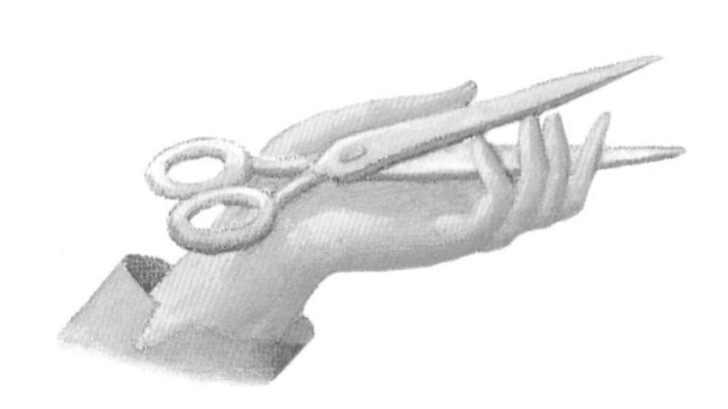

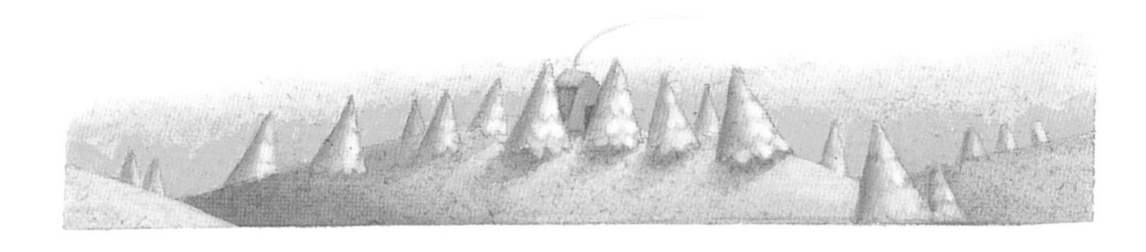

On she walked through a year and a day, until one evening she spied a third cottage with a wisp of smoke rising up through the trees. There she came across an old woman drawing water from a well.

"Pardon me, mother," said the Princess, "but have you seen a great white bear, heading for a land that lies east of the sun and west of the moon? I think he might have passed this way."

The old woman nodded, "Here he came and now he's gone. That way he went, but you'll never catch him." The old woman pointed into the thick of the forest.

"There I go, late or never," the Princess sighed and as she turned to leave the old woman called out, "If you are traveling to the land that lies east of the sun and west of the moon, you had better take this with you," and she handed the Princess a golden cup. The Princess thanked her and tucked the cup into the folds of her skirt.

On and on the Princess walked until she heard the sound of children weeping and crying. There in a clearing she came across a tumbledown cottage nestled at the base of a huge glass mountain. Outside the cottage stood a woman in rags and tatters, filling a cooking pot with stones.

"Pardon me, mother," said the Princess, "but have you seen a great white bear, heading for a land that lies east of the sun and west of the moon? I think he might have passed this way."

"The white bear? Yes, he passed this way and the place you seek lies high above, upon that mountain of glass. But you'll never catch him. For only the birds can go there. The slopes are too steep for the likes of us to climb."

Hearing this, the Princess sat down at the base of the glass mountain and she would have wept, had it not been for the cries of the hungry children who now crowded about the stone-filled pot.

"Why is it," asked the Princess, "that you feed your children stones?"

"'Tis all I have," the woman sighed. "My husband is a blacksmith and he's off working and we've eaten the cupboards bare."

Then a feeling of great compassion filled the Princess, and she drew her gifts from her skirt. She spread the tablecloth and a great feast appeared before them. She passed the cup from child to child and each drank its fill of milk, and then she sat and clipped the scissors this way and that, until all the children were warmly dressed in brightly colored clothes.

The woman thanked the Princess kindly and promised her a favor in return.

And so it was that when the blacksmith returned, he forged great iron claws for the Princess's hands and her feet.

The very next day, the Princess began to climb the great mountain of glass, daring neither to look up nor down. Higher and higher she climbed and the air grew cold and the sky dark. Her arms and legs ached and her hands were torn and bloody. And when she thought she could not climb any further she came to a land where the sky was thick with dark clouds, and the land was all bare brown hills, creased by a winding road.

Following the road, the Princess came at last to a great, gray castle. This was the home of the Troll Queen. The Princess sat outside the castle walls and reaching into the folds of her skirt she pulled out the tablecloth and flicked it one way and then the other, so that a great feast spread itself all about her.

The smell of the food brought the Troll Queen to her window, and spying the magic cloth she called, "Though my cooks sweat day and night, we will never have food enough for the wedding feast. What will you take for your fine toy?"

And the Princess replied, "It is not for sale for gold or money. But I will give it to you in return for one night with the Prince, your bridegroom."

The Troll Queen agreed, but she was a cunning creature, and that night she slipped a sleeping draught into the Prince's wine. When the Princess was led to the bedchamber, the Prince lay in a thick, dreamless slumber.

Then the Princess wept and cried,

"Three long years I've searched for you,

My gift of cloth I've sold for you,

A mountain of glass I climbed for you,

Will you not wake and turn to me?"

But the Prince did not wake and in the morning the guards tossed her out through the castle gates.

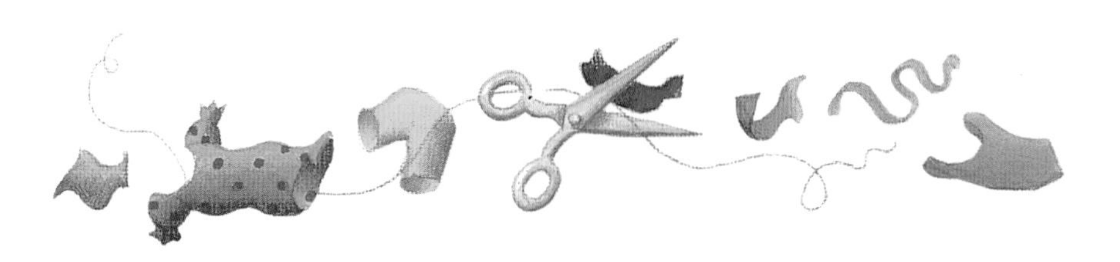

Again the Princess sat outside the walls of the castle and reached into the folds of her skirt, pulling out the silver scissors. SNIP, SNAP, SNIP she cut through the air, and brightly colored clothes fell about her feet.

The flash and click of the silver brought the Troll Queen to her window, and spying the silver scissors she called, "Though my tailors toil day and night, we will never clothe the wedding party in time. What is the price for your fine toy?"

And the Princess replied, "It is not for sale for gold or money. But I will give it to you in return for another night with the Prince, your bridegroom."

The Troll Queen agreed, but again she slipped a sleeping draught into the Prince's wine. So when the Princess was led to the bridegroom's chamber, he could not be woken from his slumber.

Then the Princess wept and cried,

"Three long years I've searched for you,

My gift of silver I've sold for you,

A mountain of glass I climbed for you,

Will you not wake and turn to me?"

And in the morning the guards tossed her out through the castle gates.

So for a third time the Princess sat outside the castle walls and drew from the folds of her skirt the last of her gifts, the golden cup. She tossed it, this way and that, causing wine and ale to flow.

The sweet smell of the wine brought the Troll Queen to her window, and spying the golden cup she called, "Though my brewers work day and night, we will never have drink enough for the wedding feast. What will you take for your fine toy?"

And the Princess replied, "It is not for sale for gold or money. But I will give it to you in return for one last night with the Prince, your bridegroom."

The Troll Queen agreed, and prepared a sleeping draught.

But a kindly servant of the Prince, who for the last two nights had heard the Princess's cries, told his master of the young woman's weeping. So when the Troll Queen gave the Prince his wine, he just pretended to drink it and then lay still as if he had fallen into a deep sleep.

But the Troll Queen grew suspicious. To check that the sleeping draught had worked, she gave the Prince a long hard pinch in the arm. But even though the pain was terrible, the Prince did not flinch.

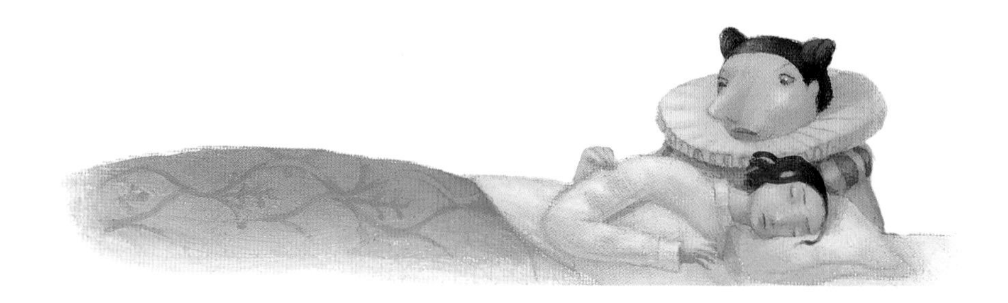

That night when the Princess knelt by his bed she wept,

"Three long years I've searched for you,

My gift of gold I've sold for you,

A mountain of glass I climbed for you,

Will you not wake and turn to me?"

And when her hot tears fell upon his face the Prince opened his eyes and they embraced, and their embrace was sweet and long and true.

"Listen, my love," whispered the Prince, "tomorrow, I am promised to marry the Troll Queen, if she can first wash the wax stains from my wedding shirt. Hide yourself among the wedding guests, for only my true bride will be able to wash the shirt clean."

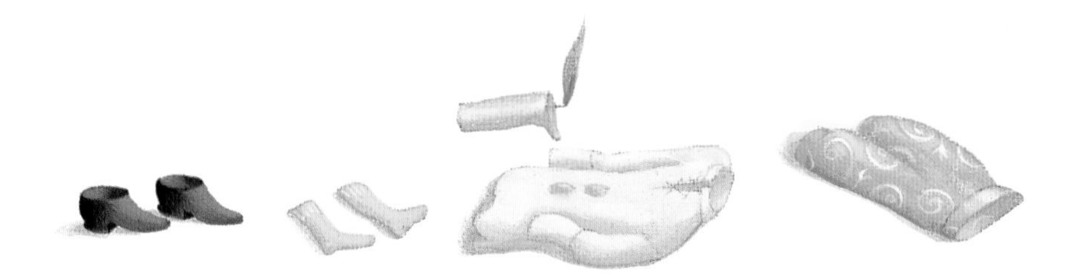

The next morning the wedding party assembled by the river, and the Princess stood quietly among them. The Prince held his stained shirt out to the Troll Queen, calling that only his true bride would be able to wash the shirt clean.

Snorting with impatience, the Troll Queen stepped forward and snatched the stained shirt, plunging it into the water. But the more she rubbed, the larger and darker the stains grew. And she scowled and spat with anger and threw the shirt on the ground.

Then the Princess stepped from the crowd and dipped the shirt in the river and instantly it was clean and bride-white. And as the Princess held the shirt high for all to see, the sun burst through the dark clouds, turning the Troll Queen and all her followers into cold, gray stone.

The Prince and the Princess flew from the land that lay east of the sun and west of the moon, taking with them many treasures. And when they returned to the Prince's castle, they called for the Princess's family. And a wedding feast was held that lasted for seven days and seven nights, the likes of which had never been seen before.

With food enough for gods and paupers,
Music that called trees to dance,
Wine enough to fill an ocean
And luck enough for all to chance.

The Prince and Princess lived happily ever after. And so may we.

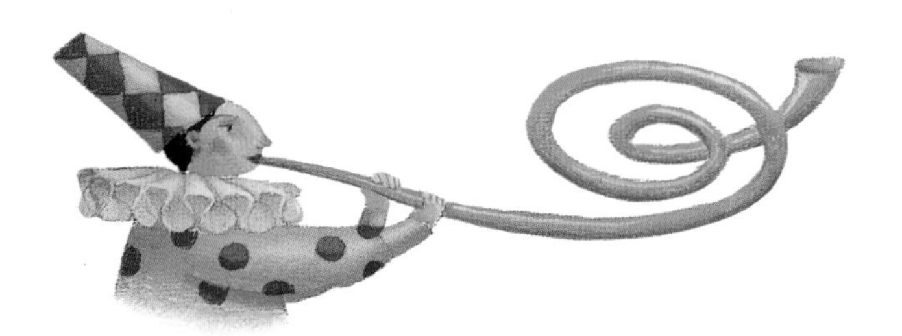

Afterword

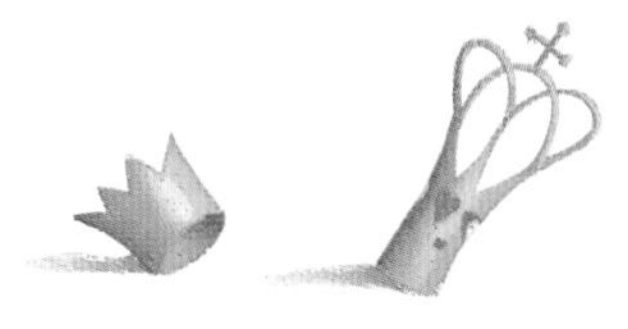

The Princess and the White Bear King combines the themes of three classic wonder tales: *East of the Sun, West of the Moon, The Black Bull of Norraway* and *The White Bear King.* All of these tales are firmly rooted in the folk tradition of Northern Europe, but the origins of *East of the Sun, West of the Moon* lie in one of the most potent and famous of love stories, the Greek myth of Eros and Psyche. When she earns the wrath of Aphrodite, having been favorably compared to the goddess of love on account of her beauty, Psyche is told by the oracle at Delphi that she must share her life on a lonely mountaintop with a monster bridegroom. But instead of being marooned in a monster's lair, she is spirited away to an enchanted palace. Here, she is visited at night by a tender lover, but never allowed to look upon his face. Eventually, taking the advice of her jealous sisters, she uses an oil lamp to discover her companion's true identity. To her astonishment, she sees the beautiful god of love, Eros, son of Aphrodite. Eros wakens from his sleep, curses Psyche for her lack of trust and leaves her, declaring "where there is no trust, there can be no love." To win him back, Psyche must perform a series of seemingly impossible tasks set for her by Aphrodite. Finally, the couple are happily reunited.

The theme of the animal bridegroom is a recurrent fairy tale motif, and famously appears in *Beauty and the Beast* and in *The Black Bull of Norraway*, a story that shares many themes with East of the Sun, West of the Moon. Here, the heroine also has three charms that she must use to gain access to her lost companion, and she is also tested by having to climb a glass mountain and wash clean his shirt. I first came across *The Black Bull of Norraway* as a child, and to this day hold the tale responsible for my yearning to ride around the countryside of New Zealand on a large, black bull.

The Princess and the White Bear King also draws on another Norwegian folk tale, *The White Bear King.* I first encountered this story in Kenya, where I was vividly reminded of the power of story to transform and transport, as the audience sat sweating on the dry, dusty shores of Lake Victoria, our minds inhabiting the frozen and windswept north! In my story, I have included the opening of *The White Bear King*, with a princess who dreams of a golden crown. I have also incorporated the princess's journey through the forest and encounter with the blacksmith's children, both from variants of *The White Bear King*, as these incidents attracted me more than the journey in *East of the Sun, West of the Moon.* To me, that account emphasizes the outward-facing masculine world of achievement and conquest of the natural world, whereas I wanted to highlight the feminine aspect of the heroine's journey, basing it more in relationship and feeling – for the Princess needs these qualities just as much as the powers of perseverance and endurance, conveyed by her long walk and by her climb up the glass mountain, in order to win back her lost Prince.

I have performed this story many times and it remains a favorite with audiences the world over. The story begins with a dream, as do so many of our adventures in life, and ends as all fairy tales should, with laughter, love and happiness ever after.

Tanya Robyn Batt,
New Zealand, 2004

At Barefoot Books, we celebrate art and story that opens the hearts and minds of children from all walks of life, inspiring them to read deeper, search further, and explore their own creative gifts. Taking our inspiration from many different cultures, we focus on themes that encourage independence of spirit, enthusiasm for learning, and sharing of the world's diversity. Interactive, playful and beautiful, our products combine the best of the present with the best of the past to educate our children as the caretakers of tomorrow.

Live Barefoot!
Join us at www.barefootbooks.com